Estimados padres de familia,

Están a punto de comenzar una emocionante aventura con su hijo y nosotros ¡seremos su guía!

Su misión es: Convertir a su hijo en un lector.

Nuestra misión: Hacerlo divertido.

LEVEL UP! READERS les da oportunidades para lectura independiente para todos los niños, comenzando con aquellos que ya saben el abecedario. Nuestro programa tiene una estructura flexible que hará que los nuevos lectores se sientan emocionados y que alcancen sus logros, no aburridos o frustrados. Los Niveles de Lectura Guiada en la parte posterior de cada libro serán su guía para encontrar el nivel adecuado. ¿Cómo comenzar?

Cada nivel de lectura desarrolla nuevas habilidades:

Nivel 1: PREPARANDO: Desde conocer el abecedario hasta decifrar palabras.
lenguaje básico – repetición – claves visuales
Niveles de Lectura Guiada: aa, A, B, C, D

Nivel 2: MEJORANDO: Desde decifrar palabras individuales hasta leer oraciones completas.
palabras comúnes – oraciones cortas – cuentos sencillos
Niveles de Lectura Guiada: C, D, E, F, G

Nivel 3: A JUGAR: Desde leer oraciones sencillas hasta disfrutar cuentos completos.
nuevas palabras – temas comúnes – historias divertidas
Niveles de Lectura Guiada: F, G, H, I, J, K

Nivel 4: EL RETO: Navega por oraciones complejas y aprende nuevo vocabulario.
vocabulario interesante – oraciones más largas – cuentos emocionantes
Niveles de Lectura Guiada: H, I, J, K, L, M

Nivel 5: EXPLORA: Prepárate para leer libros en capítulos.
capítulos cortos – párrafos – historias complejas
Niveles de Lectura Guiada: K, L, M, N, O, P

¡Déle el control al lector!

Aventuras y diversión le esparan en cada nivel.

Obtenga más información en:
littlebeebooks.com/level-up-readers

Dear Parents,

You are about to begin an exciting adventure with your child, and we're here to be your guide!

Your mission: Raise a reader.

Our mission: Make it fun.

LEVEL UP! READERS provides independent reading opportunities for all children, starting with those who already know the alphabet. Our program's flexible structure helps new readers feel excited and accomplished, not bored or frustrated. The Guided Reading Level shown on the back of each book helps caregivers and educators find just the right fit. So where do you start?

Each level unlocks new skills:

Level 1: GET READY: From knowing the alphabet to decoding words.
basic language – repetition – picture clues
Guided Reading Levels: aa, A, B, C, D

Level 2: POWER UP: From decoding single words to reading whole sentences.
common words – short sentences – simple stories
Guided Reading Levels: C, D, E, F, G

Level 3: PLAY: From reading simple sentences to enjoying whole stories.
new words – popular themes – fun stories
Guided Reading Levels: F, G, H, I, J, K

Level 4: CHALLENGE: Navigate complex sentences and learn new vocabulary.
interest-based vocabulary – longer sentences – exciting stories
Guided Reading Levels: H, I, J, K, L, M

Level 5: EXPLORE: Prepare for chapter books.
short chapters – paragraphs – complex stories
Guided Reading Levels: K, L, M, N, O, P

Put the controls in the hands of the reader!

Fun and adventure await on every level.

Find out more at:
littlebeebooks.com/level-up-readers

BuzzPop®

An imprint of Little Bee Books
251 Park Avenue South, New York, NY 10010
Copyright © 2020 Disney Enterprises, Inc.
All rights reserved, including the right of reproduction
in whole or in part in any form.
BuzzPop and associated colophon are trademarks of Little Bee Books.
For information about special discounts on bulk purchases, please
contact Little Bee Books at sales@littlebeebooks.com.
Manufactured in China TPL 0520
ISBN 978-1-4998-0879-7 (pbk)
First Edition 10 9 8 7 6 5 4 3 2 1
ISBN 978-1-4998-0880-3 (hc)
First Edition 10 9 8 7 6 5 4 3 2 1

buzzpopbooks.com

THE LITTLE MERMAID

La voz de Ariel
Ariel's Voice

Adaptation by Stevie Stack
Translation by Laura Collado Píriz
Illustrated by the Disney Storybook Art Team

BuzzPOP

Ariel es una princesa sirena.
Flounder es su amigo el pez.

Ariel is a mermaid princess.
Flounder the fish is her friend.

Tambien ella es amiga de Scuttle.
Scuttle le enseña cosas sobre los
humanos a Ariel.
Ariel quiere conocer a los humanos
y ser parte de su mundo.

She is friends with Scuttle, too.
Scuttle teaches Ariel about humans.
Ariel wants to meet the humans and
be part of their world.

El rey Tritón es el padre de Ariel.
Él está enfadado con Ariel.

King Triton is Ariel's father.
He is angry with Ariel.

Él piensa que los humanos son peligrosos.

—¡Nunca volverás a la superficie de nuevo! —él dice.

He thinks humans are dangerous. "You are never to go to the surface again!" he says.

Por la noche hay una tormenta.
Ariel nada a la superficie
del agua.

At night, there is a storm.
Ariel swims to the surface
of the water.

Ella ve a un humano caerse de
un barco.
Su nombre es Príncipe Eric.

She sees a human fall off a ship.
His name is Prince Eric.

Ariel rescata a Eric.
Ella lo saca a la superficie.

Ariel rescues Eric.
She pulls him to the surface.

Ariel le canta a Eric.
Ella se enamora de él.
Ella desearía poder vivir en tierra
con él.

Ariel sings to Eric.
She falls in love with him.
She wishes she could live on land
with him.

Úrsula es una bruja del mar que
convierte a Ariel en humana para que
ella pueda estar con Eric.
Pero ella quiere la voz de Ariel
como pago.

Ursula the sea witch will turn Ariel
into a human so she can be with Eric.
But she wants Ariel's voice as
payment.

Si Eric besa a Ariel en tres días,
ella será humana para siempre.
Si no, ella pertenecerá a Úrsula.
Ariel acepta el trato de Úrsula.

If Eric kisses Ariel in three days,
then she will stay human.
If not, she will belong to Ursula.
Ariel accepts Ursula's deal.

¡Ariel es humana!
Ella nada hasta la costa con sus
nuevas piernas humanas.

Ariel is human!
She swims to the shore with her new
human legs.

Scuttle ayuda a Ariel a hacer
un vestido.

   —Si quieres ser humana, lo primero
que debes hacer es vestirte como
uno de ellos —dice Scuttle.

Scuttle helps make a dress for Ariel.
"If you want to be a human, the first
thing you have to do is dress like
one," says Scuttle.

Ariel encuentra a Eric en la costa.
Ella intenta hablar con él, pero
ella no tiene voz.

Ariel finds Eric on the shore.
She tries to talk to him, but she has
no voice.

Eric se lleva a Ariel a su castillo.

Eric brings Ariel to his castle.

Durante la cena, Ariel piensa que un
tenedor sirve para peinarse el pelo.
Eric se ríe.
¡Le gusta Ariel!

At dinner, Ariel thinks a fork
is used to comb her hair.
Eric laughs.
He likes Ariel!

El segundo día, Eric y Ariel van a
dar un paseo en barca.
Ellos casi se besan.

On the second day, Eric and Ariel go
on a boat ride.
They almost kiss.

¡Pero las anguilas de Úrsula vuelcan la barca antes de que Eric pueda besar a Ariel!

But Ursula's eels tip the boat over before Eric can kiss Ariel!

Úrsula no puede permitir que Eric
bese a Ariel.
Ella se cambia a una forma humana y
se lleva la voz de Ariel.

Ursula cannot let Eric kiss Ariel.
She changes into a human woman and
takes Ariel's voice.

Cuando Eric escucha la voz de Ariel,
él piensa que se ha enamorado de
Úrsula.
Eric se va a casar con Úrsula.

When Eric hears Ariel's voice,
he thinks he is in love with Ursula.
Eric is going to marry Ursula.

Scuttle descubre el truco de Úrsula.

—¡Ella es la bruja del mar con un disfraz! —dice Scuttle.

Scuttle discovers Ursula's trick. "She's the sea witch in disguise!" says Scuttle.

Scuttle y sus amigos detienen a
Úrsula antes de que ella pueda
casarse con Eric.

Scuttle and his friends stop Ursula
before she can marry Eric.

¡La voz de Ariel vuelve a su dueña!
Pero es demasiado tarde.

Ariel's voice returns!
But it is too late.

El tercer día acaba.
Ariel vuelve a convertirse
en una sirena.
Ella ahora pertenece a Úrsula.

The third day ends.
Ariel turns back into a mermaid.
She now belongs to Ursula.

Úrsula se transforma en
un monstruo gigantesco.
¡Ella ataca!
Eric la detiene para siempre.

Ursula transforms into
a huge monster.
She attacks!
Eric stops her for good.

El rey Tritón ve que Ariel está
enamorada de Eric.
Y él la vuelve a convertir en humana.

King Triton sees that Ariel is
in love with Eric.
He turns her back into a human.

Ariel vuelve con Eric.
Eric también ama a Ariel.
Y ellos viven felices para siempre.

Ariel returns to Eric.
Eric loves Ariel, too.
They live happily ever after.

¿Te diste cuenta?

El verbo "**besar**" cambia durante la historia. Por ejemplo:

"Si Eric **besa** a Ariel en tres días, ella será humana para siempre."

"Úrsula no puede permitir que Eric **bese** a Ariel."

En las dos frases, no sabemos si Eric besará Ariel.

En la primera frase, una acción depende de la otra. Ariel no puede ser humana para siempre si Eric no la **besa**. Usamos "si" para mostrar que el beso podría ocurrir o no.

En la segunda frase, la primera acción convierte la otra acción en un deseo, duda o posibilidad. En vez de "Eric **besa** a Ariel", decimos "que Eric **bese** a Ariel" para mostrar que solo es una posibilidad.

Did you notice?

The verb "**kiss**" changes throughout the story. For example:

"If Eric **kisses** Ariel in three days, then she will stay human."

"Ursula cannot let Eric **kiss** Ariel."

In both sentences, we don't know if Eric will kiss Ariel.

In the first sentence, one action depends on the other. Ariel cannot stay human unless Eric **kisses** her. We use "if" to show that the kiss may or may not happen.

In the second sentence, the first action turns the other action into a wish, doubt, or possibility. Instead of "Eric **kisses** Ariel," we say "Eric **kiss** Ariel" to show that it is only a possibility.

Glosario

Un trato es cuando dos o más personas aceptan a hacer, decir o intercambiar algo.

Un disfraz es cualquier cosa que lleves puesto o hagas para esconder quién eres.

Una sirena es una criatura marina con la cabeza y parte superior del cuerpo de una mujer y la cola de un pez.

Rescatar es liberar o salvar a alguien.

La costa es la parte de tierra justo al lado del mar.

Transformar es cambiar una característica de personalidad o apariencia física.

¿Qué otras palabras nuevas aprendiste?

Glossary

A deal is when two or more people agree to do, say, or trade something.

A disguise is anything someone wears or does to hide who they are.

A mermaid is a sea creature with the head and upper body of a woman and the tail of a fish.

To rescue is to free or save someone.

The shore is the piece of land right next to the sea.

To transform is to change a personal characteristic or physical appearance.

What other new words did you learn?